Say Boo to the Animals!

to the

Ian Whybrow   Tim Warnes

Say Boo
to the
Animals!

MACMILLAN CHILDREN'S BOOKS

Ready, steady, off we go!
Creep through the woods on tippy-toe.

We're off to meet some animals, and when we do
If you see a scary one, just say **BOO!**

There's an owl, up a tree.
I wonder if he's after me?

To-whit!
To-whoo!

We're not scared of you, **BOO**!

Help, a monster's on the loose!
Quick! Say boo to the mighty moose.

Stamp!

Stamp!

Stamp!

We're not scared of you, **BOO**!

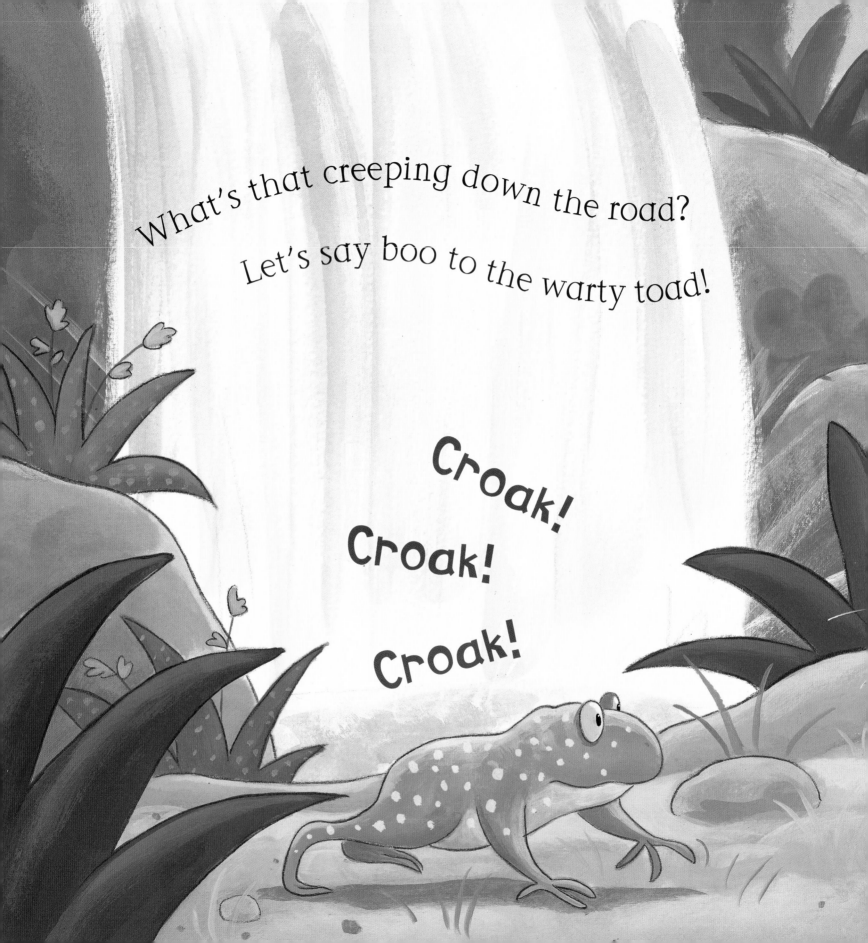

What's that creeping down the road?

Let's say boo to the warty toad!

Croak!
Croak!
Croak!

We're not scared of you, **BOO!**

Here's a thumper and a thriller!

Now say boo to the giant gorilla!

Thump!

This is where the tiger lies.
Let's give him a big surprise!

We're not scared of you, **BOO!**

Baby wolf cub wants to play.
He's not scary – he can stay!

Just in case you're not quite sure
Let's hear your loudest **BOO** once more.

For my *vicini cari* the Viazzani children, Valentina, Adelaide,
Emilia and Giacomo – who will all please read this in turn to
Clementina until she is *annoiata fino alle lacrime* or *blu nella faccia.*

I.W.

For Jacob, with love from Uncle Tim!

T.W.

First published 2012 by Macmillan Children's Books
an imprint of Pan Macmillan
20 New Wharf Road. London N1 9RR
Associated companies throughout the world
www.panmacmillan.com

ISBN: 978-1-5098-2912-5

Text copyright © Ian Whybrow 2012
Illustrations copyright © Tim Warnes 2012

You can find out more about Tim Warnes's books at www.chapmanandwarnes.com

The right of Ian Whybrow and Tim Warnes to be identified
as the author and illustrator of this work has been asserted by them
in accordance with the Copyright. Designs and Patents Act 1988.

1 3 5 7 9 8 6 4 2

A CIP catalogue record for this book is available
from the British Library.

Printed in China

The inclusion of author website addresses in this book does not constitute an endorsement
by or association with Macmillan Publishers of such sites or the content. products.
advertising or other materials presented on such sites.